Dragon Tuesday

AMY LAURENS

OTHER WORKS

SANCTUARY SERIES

Where Shadows Rise
Through Roads Between
When Worlds Collide

KADITEOS SERIES

How Not To Acquire A Castle
How Not To Ring The Hero's Bell
How Not To Take Over The World

SHORT STORY COLLECTIONS

Of Sea Foam and Blood
Darkness and Good

NON-FICTION

How To Write Dogs
How To Theme
How To Create Cultures

Find other works by the author at
www.amylaurens.com

dragon tuesday

INKLET #13

AMY LAURENS

Inkprint PRESS

www.inkprintpress.com

Print ISBN: 978-1-925825-12-1
eBook ISBN: 9781386899501

www.inkprintpress.com

National Library of Australia Cataloguing-in-Publication Data
Laurens, Amy 1985 –
Dragon Tuesday
34 p.
ISBN: 978-1-925825-12-1
Inkprint Press, Canberra, Australia
1. Fiction—Fantasy—Dark Fantasy 2. Fiction—Short Stories 3. Fiction—Fantasy—Dragons & Mythical Creatures

First Print Edition: July 2019
Cover design © Inkprint Press
Interior art © Amy Laurens

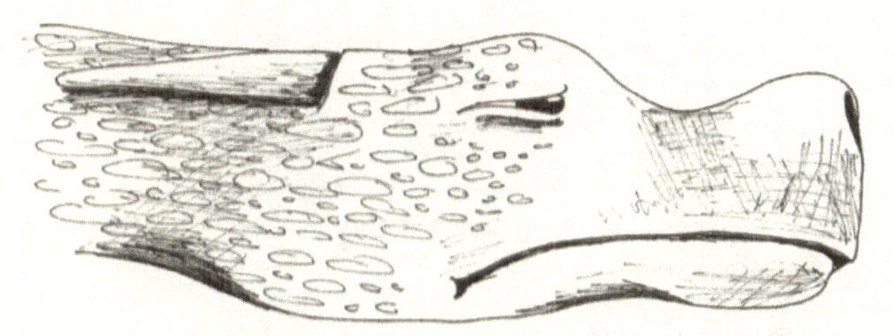

DRAGON TUESDAY

How can you help? Heh. I'd love to know. More than you, probably. But I doubt you can. I mean sure, you're more than welcome to try—I'm not keen on being stuck like this forever, and presumably they found some way to help my great grandmother.

No, not stuck as in up the tree, I know how to climb out of a tree, *thank* you. I mean like *this*, in this body.

Well yes, I suppose it is pretty, in a way. But it's not... me.

It *was* my great grandmother, actually. Yeah, I know that's creepy.

Uh, sure, you can touch the scales. If you can reach. Here, if I lower my tail you can probably reach.

I dunno, they're *probably* magical. I really have no idea, though.

Oh look, just let me tell you the whole story. Sit down.

Comfy? Okay.

It was a hot, sultry Tuesday with dust thick in your throat, like all of them had been in that month full of Dragon Tuesdays, and Sham and I were heading out for ice cream. There's this great little parlour at the end of Beech Avenue that does the real, genuine home-made stuff.

Although we never said it, I knew we were both hoping that this time, *we'd* be the ones to spot the dragon— the dragon that had appeared with perfect regularity, every Tuesday of that month, somewhere around our tiny town.

Seeing a dragon had become my entire goal in life.

Yeah, I know. Ironic.

So, we were walking down Main, kicking up the red dirt of the road, laughing and joking and generally having a good time. School was out, summer was on its way, and life was good.

We hit the ice cream parlour—I got raspberry coconut swirl, just for a change—and took our waffle cones outside. There we were, licking our ice creams, giggling and hot and sticky, minding no one but ourselves, glancing casually around every now and then, just in case.

I'd gotten down to the cone and almost given up hope when there was an almighty crash-thud. A blinding flash of light shone from a side street; we ditched our cones and ran towards it.

"Dragon," Sham exclaimed, eyes all lit up.

I nodded. A great beast, it was said to be, about the size of a wagon, metallic and boxy and roaring and blowing smoke out its end.

Right as we came around the corner, there was another almighty roar, and there, before our eyes, was the dragon.

We were shocked, but not half as shocked as we were when there was a clunk-clunk, and the dragon's body started opening up.

I shrank back around the corner and clutched at Sham's arm.

But that wasn't even the strangest: as the dragon's body opened up, *people* emerged. Three of them: two men and a woman. They were wearing strange clothes that gleamed, dark and form-fitting. They stared around at the squat brick buildings and murmured to themselves.

Mayor Francis must've heard the noise, 'coz he came striding out of the Hall across the street, moustache twitching. He ignored us and marched right up to the dragon riders. "And who are you?" he demanded.

Sham and I didn't hear their answer, so we edged closer.

They said something about there being a leak in time where they came from, so whenever people drove through this one area, they ended up somewhere else entirely—often here.

My first thought was, *How can time leak?* It's not like there's a tap full of it somewhere, a great space-tap full of time that's running and dripping until one day, it all runs out…

Weird.

I thought they were a bit you-know in the head, personally. Still, it was the most interesting thing Sham or I had ever seen, so we followed them.

Tailed them around from sun up 'til sundown, mostly without them knowing, while they wandered around town "taking in the sights"—which seemed to mean a lot of staring and pointing and holding up these shiny little rectangles and posing in front of them.

Things were great until they'd been there about a week.

Actually yeah, it was exactly a week; I know 'coz it was Tuesday again. They'd been driving around in that silver beast of theirs, which had turned out not to be a dragon at all—we heard them call a 'car' a couple of time—and when they stopped at the old theatre, they left the back open.

They didn't know we was there, of course, or they prolly would've made sure it was locked up real tight. But they didn't, and Sham and I knew opportunity when we saw it, so in we climbed.

We had a good poke around, bouncing on the seats and hanging out the windows—and then I found it.

It was stuffed under one of the seats, and I saw it pretty easily 'coz in the darkness of the under-seat, it *sparkled*. I pulled it out just as Sham hissed at me to shut up, they were coming, get out—and I stuffed it in my pocket without even thinking, and promptly forgot about it as we scurried away, with the 'car' riders pelting things at us.

It wasn't until after dinner, up in my own room, that I pulled it out. It reminded me of the empty lizard skins I'd seen out near the creek, cast off when the lizard grew too big for it. Except this must've come from a huge lizard.

It was paper-thin, but strong, and the whole thing had wadded up into a ball the size of two of my fists—but when I shook it out, it was nearly as tall as I was.

I draped around me, wondering for a moment what it'd be like to be a lizard. The skin was soft, flexible. And the colours…

I twirled and it swung out, sparkling iridescent in the dim evening light.

As I slowed, the skin closed over my shoulders; it fit so well. It seemed like the most natural thing in the world to stick my feet through the holes that appeared, to wrap it tight around me, to hug it around my chest—

Until the pain.

I screamed. I screamed until my throat hurt, and then I screamed until I couldn't scream anymore, even though I wanted to.

The pain, everywhere—it was insane. Intense. The most horrible thing I've ever felt or imagined.

Mum burst in and the look on her face was more terrifying than anything else.

"Oh, Chay," she said, dropping to her knees. "Oh, Chay."

"What?" I tried to say. "What is it?" But it came out as a strange sort of rasp. Panicked, I looked down at my hands—only they weren't hands. They were claws. Like a lizard, only bigger and a shining, grey with a rainbow iridescence.

Just like the skin.

So Mum took me down to the kitchen and explained: my great grandmother had been the last of the real dragons, creatures half the size of a horse with wide, ethereal wings and a long scaly tail.

When she'd become the very last dragon—when her husband had been murdered—she'd done the only thing she could: she'd shed her skin and taken the form of a human. She'd remarried, had my mother—and my mother had had me.

And I'd somehow gotten my hands on the skin. And because my grandmother's blood flows through my veins, the skin was able to transform me.

Mum told me all this, and for a moment I was shocked.

Then I was just plain horrified, terror settling in my gut like a stone.

I raced away, half running, half flying, an odd sort of skipping gait that was mostly a stumble.

I didn't have any idea where I was going; I just ran, maybe hoping I could outrun my fate. I'd wanted to *see* a dragon; not become one.

In my panic, I ran right into the strangers. They took one look at me, and started screaming and hugging each other. "Our dragon!" they shouted. "We found it!"

Something even scarier than learning I was a dragon? Learning that I wasn't the only dragon hunter in town.

My heart pounded and I raced off again, barely ahead of them and losing ground.

The woman snatched at my tail and I leapt into the air in fright—which is about the time I realised what my new wings could actually do. I flew, circling up and away, and their cries died down behind me.

I could have flown away right then. It might have saved poor Sham if I had.

But maybe not. And anyway, I didn't, so never mind.

I hid that night in the barn out of the back of my house. From up in the loft I could see the light in the kitchen, and every now and then Mum's silhouette passed by, and I could see her, and feel a little bit like I was home.

I was drifting off when I heard the door creak open, and with my new night vision and sense of smell, I could tell that it was Sham.

I opened my mouth to speak—but another voice beat me to it.

"Where is she?"

It was one of the strangers, the tallest man—the scary one.

Sham froze. "I… I don't know."

"Come now," said the woman, slinking over to him. "We know it's her we want, and you know it too. Just tell us where she is, and everything will be all right."

Sham twitched.

Please, no, I thought desperately. *Don't tell them.*

He didn't. He stared back at them, fists clenched, and said, "I don't know what you're talking about. I don't know nothing."

I thought at the time he was pretty brave. Now I'm not sure if he was brave, or just a little stupid.

But either way, the man had enough. "We saw the dragon!" he yelled, right in Sham's face. "We recognized our skin! You stole it, you and that girl. We know you're friends; we *know* you know where she is, and you're going to take us to her. Right. Now."

He hit Sham as he said those last words, smashing a sparking rod across his head and shoulders again and again.

Right then, I realized how much I'd loved having Sham for a friend. He'd been there for me when no one else had, and hadn't even laughed that afternoon when he'd seen me in my skin. He'd been the best friend a girl could ask for.

And if they didn't stop soon, they'd kill him for it.

I shivered, wanting to do something, but knowing I was too small and powerless to do a thing. I couldn't even cry as I watched them beat him to a pulp.

He didn't get up again.

And, to my shame, I never moved until they were gone.

That… that's it, really. I ran, and I flew, and I hid. And I got lost. I'm not proud of that. Not at all.

But I don't know where I came from, and I have no idea where to go. So here I am. A shiny little dragon, the very thing I always wanted to see, hiding in a tree, with no friends, and no future, reduced to letting random strangers pet my tail, because sometimes then they feed me.

Why are you laughing? It's really not that funny.

No, it isn't!

No, I don't recognise you at all—

Um, I think you should put that down. No, I really think you should put that—

THE MAKING OF
DRAGON TUESDAY

Oddly enough, it's the ice cream that always stands out to me most in this story. It's a very specific memory of some time my husband and I spent in Paris back in 2009, when the weather was hot and the gelato was superlative.

The second thing that stands out to me when I remember this story is the glimmering, iridescent dragon skin that our main character finds in the car, that image of something shiny dangerously in a dark crevice, magic in a mundane place, temptation, beautiful and alluring...

The third thing is the image of the car, rusting and belching smoke and in need of a good mechanic, somehow appearing through space and time in the red-dust street of the sleepy little town where nothing is every supposed to happen. The collision of worlds, the frenetic glee of the time/space travellers at discovering their car actually *worked…*

This is another one of those stories where I'm entirely uncertain whether or not it all came together in the end, but I love it still, because of those images: the ice cream, the shimmer, the rustbox in a red dirt street. You can practically feel the heat, taste the suffocation, breathe the claustrophobia as the dragon skin closes over you.

And sometimes, in life, we feel just like that, when we've learned too late what Chay learned:

That all that glitters is not gold— and the thing that we seek isn't always the thing that's best for us.

DOWNLOAD YOUR FREE EBOOK

When you buy a print book from Inkprint Press, we like to say THANK YOU by offering you the ebook for free!

Please head to
www.inkprintpress.com/inklets/13/
and the use the coupon INK13 to get your copy of this Inklet in epub AND mobi today!
(Coupon will only work once.)

Read more by this author!

OF SEA FOAM AND BLOOD: TO DUST

Sometimes running away is the hardest thing you can do. What I want, what I really want, is to turn around right now and plunge back into the midst of the Maliche, let their rotting, stinking bodies surround me, and kill as many as I can before I die. For Mum. For Dad. For Joss.

God, please let Joss get away. Mum and Dad might be gone, but please, please… save him. I left him climbing for a rooftop, and the Maliche can't climb, and he might be safe enough— but I have to run, and running is so, so hard when all you want to do is die.

I can't die though, not today. Today I have to live, because in my backpack, weighing me down like guilt, is the box. It's a perfect cube I can balance on one hand, sharp-edged and shined to perfection—a magic box, the only hope we have of stopping the Maliche forever. And I want to stop them more than anything else in the world, more than I want to die, because while there are Maliche, no one dies.

And so I run, heading north in a town that runs south towards the battle, running for life and death and salvation along a road whipped by the wind and smogged with dust.

From dust created, to dust returned. Only that's exactly it: with the Maliche on our doorstep, there is no return. I've seen the bodies they leave behind, twisted, gruesome things with flesh squeezed until the insides pop, left in the sun to ferment with a rictus of pain on their faces.

And the eyes. The eyes are the worst.

No. Running away is hard, but it must be done. Humanity needs to die.

Keep reading! Head to
http://www.amylaurens.com/books/short-stories/of-sea-foam-and-blood/
to buy your copy now!

ABOUT THE AUTHOR

AMY LAURENS is an Australian author of fantasy fiction for all ages. She's never been a dragon, but she does particularly love a good ice cream.

Amy has written a middle grade fantasy trilogy (the *Sanctuary* series), and this year (2019) her comedic fantasy trilogy is coming out, starting with *How Not To Acquire A Castle*.

You can find out more about Amy at her website, www.amylaurens.com.

INKLET #007
SEVENTY
LIANA BROOKS

INKLET #008
A Final Request for Mercy
AMY LAURENS

INKLET #009
the kitten psychologist
vs.
the kitten's owners
THEA VAN DIEPEN

Answer the Question
AMY LAURENS

Happily, Red
AMY LAURENS

INKLET #012
the kitten psychologist
tries to be patient
through email
THEA VAN DIEPEN

INKLET #013
DRAGON Tuesday
AMY LAURENS

INKLET #014
RED PLANET REFUGEES
LIANA BROOKS

INKLET #015
the kitten psychologist &
What The Kitten Did
THEA VAN DIEPEN

INKLET #016
Cherry Blossom
AMY LAURENS

Alone
AMY LAURENS

INKLET #018
the kitten psychologist
& The Kitten
Come To A Conclusion
THEA VAN DIEPEN

INKLET #019
LEVEL NINE
LIANA BROOKS

INKLET #020
To Dust
AMY LAURENS

INKLET #021
Interchange
AMY LAURENS

INKLET #022
Emalia's Lanterns
LIANA BROOKS

INKLET #023
Dear Santa
AMY LAURENS

INKLET #024
The Quilt-Maker's Scrap
AMY L. LAURENS

www.ingramcontent.com/pod-product-compliance
Lightning Source LLC
Chambersburg PA
CBHW051303190726
48286CB00004B/1234